Walking in the Sky

"Polly's Adventure"

Paulette Tomasson

Balboa Press books may be ordered through booksellers or by contacting:

Balboa Press
A Division of Hay House
1663 Liberty Drive
Bloomington, IN 47403
www.balboapress.com
1 (877) 407-4847

Because of the dynamic nature of the Internet, any web addresses or links contained in this book may have changed since publication and may no longer be valid. The views expressed in this work are solely those of the author and do not necessarily reflect the views of the publisher, and the publisher hereby disclaims any responsibility for them.

ISBN: 978-1-9822-1662-7 (sc)
ISBN: 978-1-9822-1661-0 (e)

Print information available on the last page.

Balboa Press rev. date: 12/11/2019

BALBOA.
PRESS
A DIVISION OF HAY HOUSE

To Kimberley, always a sense of joy.

Once there was a little girl named Polly who lived on the prairie.

She was the only seven-year-old in her whole village and the only child in her family.

Polly had no brothers or sisters, and she had no friends to play with.

She was very lonely. She didn't feel like she belonged with the younger children or the older children. She wasn't part of any group.

Polly was alone, which made her feel very small.

How dearly she wanted a friend, and how she ached to belong.

One cold winter evening, Polly went walking out on the snowbanks near her home.

How she loved the sound of the snow squeaking under her feet and the crackling and swooshing of the northern lights as they danced above her.

Every time she sat under the stars, she felt different—less lonely somehow.

How she loved the stars and the way they twinkled at her. How she loved the sky that seemed to go on forever.

Polly walked along the snowbanks, wishing she had a friend while talking to the stars.

Suddenly she heard a small voice. "Over here. Over here. I'm here."

Polly looked around. She couldn't see anything.

"No, down here. Look. See me."

Polly looked down. She couldn't believe her eyes!

There, by her feet, a white, sparkly little snowflake was hopping up and down.

"Be careful. Don't step on me," the snowflake squeaked.

"Oh, I won't," replied Polly. "I promise."

"What is your name?" Polly asked.

"I'm Sparkle," said the little snowflake. "I fell from the sky last night so I could come and see you, Polly. I would like to be your friend!"

Finally, a friend! Polly was very happy to hear this, and she smiled to show it.

But then Sparkle went on. "If it snows tomorrow, I will have to settle into the snowbank with my family, so I am very glad to see you tonight."

"Don't you just love how the snowflakes pile up into snowdrifts and snowbanks?"

"My snowflake family and friends have such fun together. We love it when the wind blows us around before we land. We dance and dance in the air, and then we snuggle beside one another and settle into the snowbank. It is wonderful and cozy."

"That sounds lovely," said Polly.

"But we just became friends! I was hoping you would always be here so I would not be alone."

"Don't worry, Polly; I am here now!
And I am going to take you somewhere," said Sparkle.
"Take me somewhere? Why?" asked Polly.
"There is someone you need to see. Follow me!"
And with that, little Sparkle started down the snowbank,
looking back to make sure Polly was following.

"Watch your step," she cautioned Polly.

Together, they walked to a snowdrift that looked like a door. Sparkle hopped up and down, making the secret signal.

Slowly, the snowdrift moved aside to reveal a long hallway.

"Come on!" shouted Sparkle with excitement. "Hurry!"

Down the hall they went, and soon they came into a large cave. In the middle of the room, a big throne held a large white-haired man with a long beard. He was dressed in a shiny robe and a sparkly hat.

"Welcome, Polly," he said. "I have been waiting to meet you."

"Who are you?" asked Polly.

Though she had never met him before, she immediately felt safe—just as she felt with Sparkle.

"I am Merlin," he said, "and I bring the snowy magic sparkle of winter."

He waved his wand, and the whole cave sparkled as Polly watched in amazement.

"Wow!" said Polly. "Will you be my friend?"

She had read about Merlin the magician in books, and she knew he was a special being who could do all kinds of magical things.

Merlin smiled and replied, "I know you are lonely. I am here to help you find many friends, Polly. Just maybe not the kind you were thinking of."

And then he chuckled.

Polly looked puzzled.

"I want you to look up at the sky," said Merlin.

He waved his wand, and a large circular hole appeared in the top of the cave.

It opened up so wide that they could see the stars and the northern lights dancing and sparkling above them.

Polly was excited. "Look at all the stars!" she exclaimed with her usual sense of wonder.

"Yes, I see them, Polly. And I see the moon and the northern lights. They are all so beautiful up there in the sky."

"Now, Polly, I want you to think about this. It is a very important question."

"Where does the sky begin?"

Polly looked puzzled. No one had ever asked her that before. "The sky is up there. It's up where the stars are," said Polly.

"Yes, it is," replied Merlin, "but where does it begin?" And he paused so Polly could think about her answer. "Does it begin where the stars are?"

"Does it begin where the moon is?"

"He continued to pause after each question so that Polly could think about it.

"Does it begin at the clouds? Does it begin on the mountaintops? Does it begin at the treetops?"

"Does it begin on the top of your house? Where do you think it begins?"

"Oh my," said Polly, and she peeked out at the treetops through the hole in the ceiling of the cave. Then she thought of the top of her house.

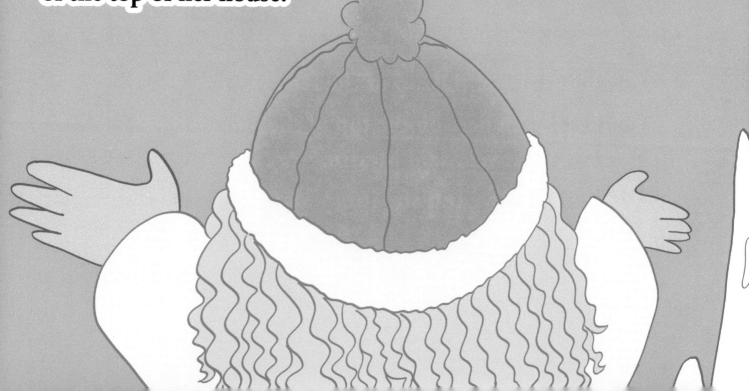

"Does it begin on the top of the fence?"

"Could it begin here on the top of the snowbank or here on the floor of the cave?" said Merlin.

"Oh," said Polly, and she jumped as she looked down at the floor.

"Oh my." She did not know how to answer the question; the sky was everywhere!

Merlin laughed. "Yes, Polly," he said, chuckling. "Think about it; you are sitting in the sky."

Polly's eyes grew big with amazement. "Really?" she asked. "Really?"

"Yes," said Merlin with a smile. "Feel it around you, Polly. You are part of the sky family."

"You are part of the stars and the moon and the planets and the northern lights."

"The clouds and even me and Sparkle and all the other snowflakes and raindrops too."

"We are all part of the sky family. The birds and butterflies and bumblebees are—and so are you, Polly. See all your new friends who are in the sky."

"But I don't fly," said Polly, and indeed she did not.

Merlin chuckled. "No, you don't fly, but you walk. You walk in the sky just as all the animals do—cats and dogs and rabbits and even elephants."

"You are a sky child. Look up, Polly. See what you are part of. Feel the sky around you. It's like a big hug."

Polly sat and looked up and around her. The stars seemed to be twinkling at her, and the northern lights seemed to be inviting her to dance with them.

"Now, get up and walk around," said Merlin. "Try it out."

Slowly, she put her feet down and opened her arms. She could feel the sky around her.

She took a very careful first step. Her eyes got bigger and bigger.

She felt the sky all around her. It *was* like a big hug!

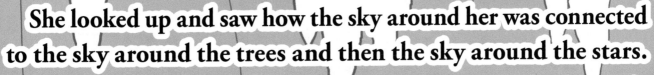

She looked up and saw how the sky around her was connected to the sky around the trees and then the sky around the stars.

Oh wow, **she thought.** *This is amazing. I am part of the sky family. I am in the sky with the stars and the birds and even the dragonflies and the ladybugs! I am a sky child.*

"Remember this," said Merlin.

Polly walked and continued to feel her connection.

It was magical, and she knew she was part of something amazing.

How she loved it!

She started to giggle with excitement and looked at Merlin.

"This is wonderful! I am a sky child. I am part of the sky family," she said with amazement.

How different everything looked and felt now.

And Polly knew she would never be the same.

"Look over there," said Merlin, "on the wall."
Polly looked, and there etched in the wall were these words:

"Polly",
who walks in the Sky,
is a Sky Child and a
Member of Merlin's Sky Dweller's Clan.

"So other children walk in the sky too?" she asked.

"Oh yes, of course," replied Merlin. "They all can. They only have to see where it begins and then go for their walk, just as you did, Polly."

"They are all sky children like you. The wonderful sky connects us all."

Polly smiled with excitement.

Then, from far away, Polly heard her mother's voice calling her to come home. "Oh, Merlin, I have to go. Thank you for coming to see me."

"Thank you for showing me who I am. I hope it doesn't snow for a long time so I can see you every day. You and Sparkle are my best friends."

Merlin and Sparkle twinkled in the moonlight. "You're welcome, Polly. You are always welcome in our family. Now it's time for you to go home."

"Good night, Polly. Enjoy walking in the sky," Merlin said as she left the cave.

Sparkle giggled, jumped, and waved goodbye.

"Walk?" said Polly. "I'm going to skip and dance!"

And she did. Polly the sky child walked, skipped, and danced all the way home!

Not only did she have new friends, she had something even better: a sense of belonging to something very big and magical.

Now it's your turn to answer the questions!

Where does the sky begin?

Can you feel and see the sky around you?

Now slowly take your first step.

Where did you do it?

Did you do it in your imagination, or did you actually walk on the floor?

What was it like?

Congratulations! You did it.

You are a person who walks in the sky and are part of Merlin's sky family.

Your certificate is on the next page. Fill it out.

This Certifies

_____

who walks in the sky
is a
Member of

"MERLIN'S SKY DWELLING CLAN"

DATE : _____

Signed: *Merlin*

CPSIA information can be obtained
at www.ICGtesting.com
Printed in the USA
BVHW022153230121
598522BV00002B/9